HELPING YOUR BRAND-NEW READER

Here's how to make first-time reading easy and fun:

- Read the introduction at the beginning of each story aloud. Look through the pictures together so that your child can see what happens in the story before reading the words.

- Read the first page to your child, placing your finger under each word.

- Let your child touch the words and read the rest of the story. Give him or her time to figure out each new word.

- If your child gets stuck on a word, you might say, *"Try something. Look at the picture. What would make sense?"*

- If your child is still stuck, supply the right word. This will allow him or her to continue to read and enjoy the story. You might say, *"Could this word be 'ball'?"*

- Always praise your child. Praise what he or she reads correctly, and praise good tries too.

- Give your child lots of chances to read the story again and again. The more your child reads, the more confident he or she will become.

- Have fun!

First edition 2005

Library of Congress Cataloging-in-Publication Data is available.

Library of Congress Catalog Card Number 2004061845

ISBN 0-7636-2572-8

2 4 6 8 10 9 7 5 3 1

Printed in China

This book was typeset in Letraset Arta.
The illustrations were done
in watercolor.

Candlewick Press
2067 Massachusetts Avenue
Cambridge, Massachusetts 02140

visit us at www.candlewick.com

TERMITE TROUBLE

CANDLEWICK PRESS
CAMBRIDGE, MASSACHUSETTS

WRITTEN AND ILLUSTRATED BY **Kathy Caple**

Contents

TERMITE EATS

Introduction

This story is called *Termite Eats.*
It's about how Termite eats his friends'
houses and they have to get new houses.
Then Termite tries to eat Ostrich's house,
and Termite gets in trouble.

Termite eats Ladybug's house.

Ladybug gets a new house.

Termite eats Mouse's house.

Mouse gets a new house.

Termite eats Dog's house.

Dog gets a new house.

Termite eats Ostrich's house.

Termite gets a new house.

TERMITE BOUNCES

Introduction

This story is called *Termite Bounces.* It's about how Termite bounces higher and higher. Then he bounces too high and gets stuck.

Termite bounces up.

Termite comes down.

Termite bounces up.

Termite comes down.

Termite bounces and flips.

Termite comes down.

Termite bounces and flips again.

Termite stays up!

TERMITE BITES

Introduction

This story is called *Termite Bites.* It's about how Termite bites a log over and over. Soon the log looks like Termite!

Termite looks at the log.

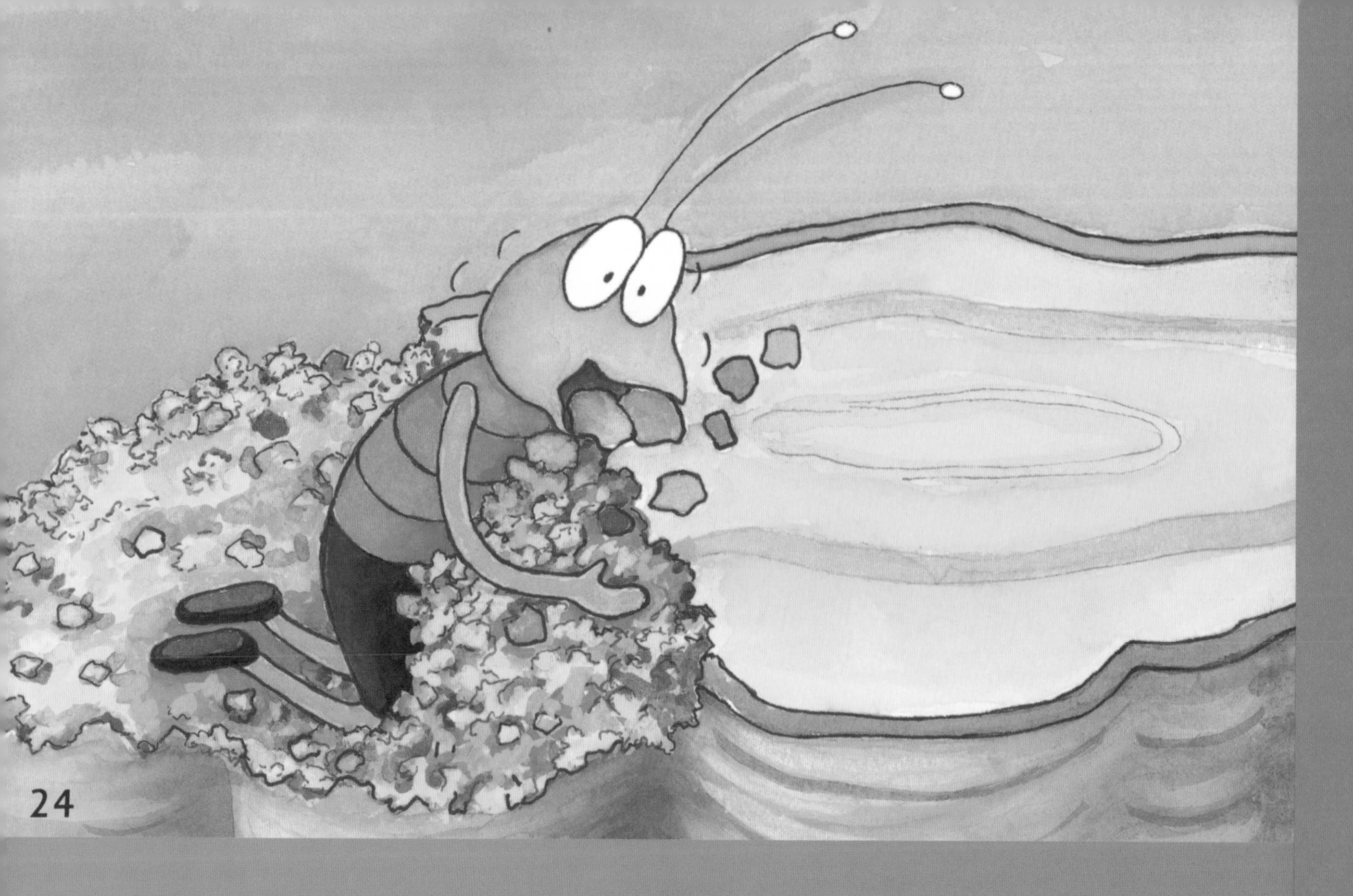

Termite bites the log.

Termite looks at the log.

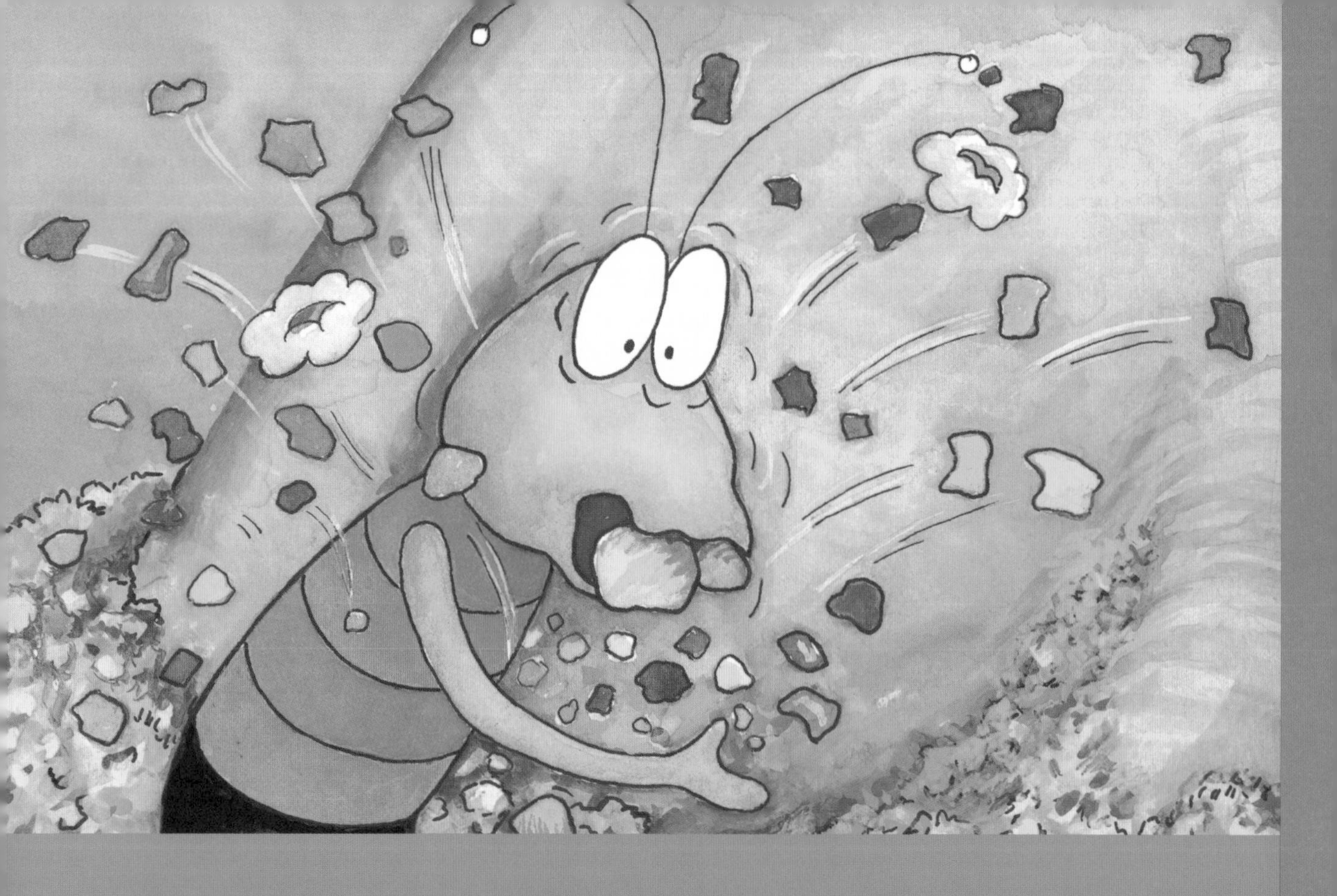

Termite bites the log.

Termite looks at the log.

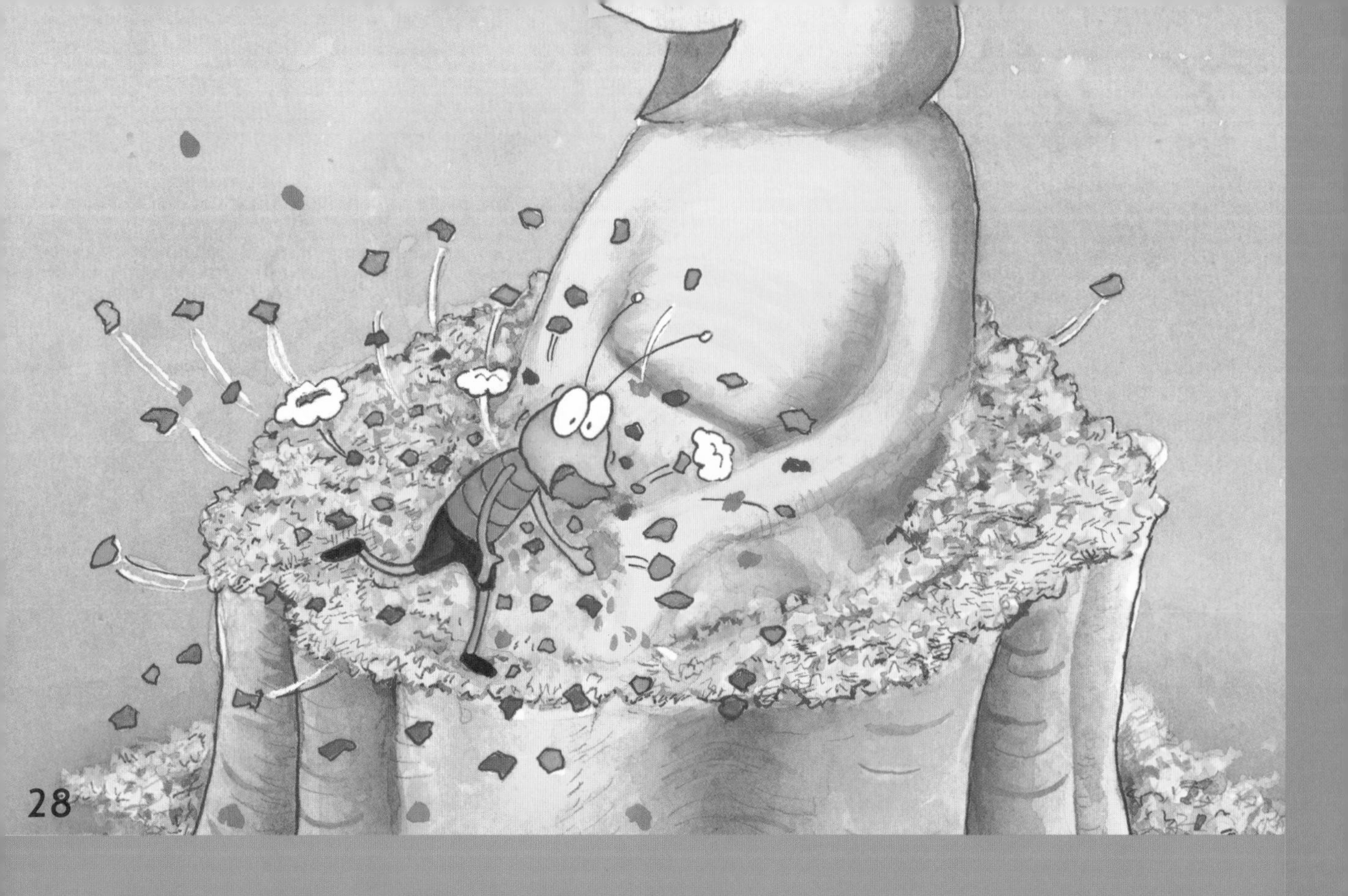

Termite bites the log.

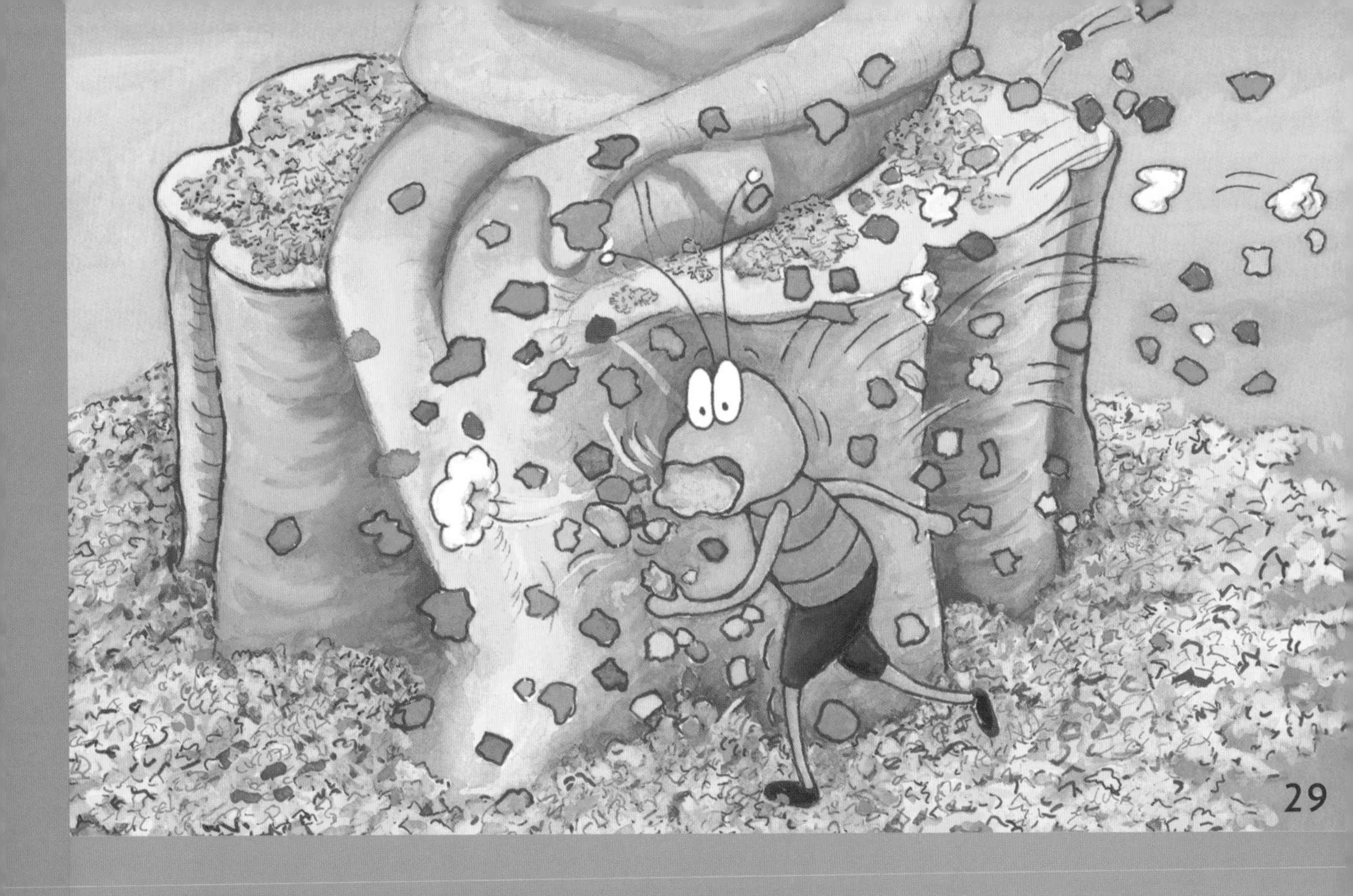

Termite bites and bites.

Termite looks at Termite.

TERMITE FLIES

Introduction

This story is called *Termite Flies*. It's about how Ostrich and Termite try to use wings to fly. Then they find a better way.

Ostrich and Termite try to fly.

CRASH!

Ostrich tries bigger wings.

CRASH!

Ostrich tries even bigger wings.

CRASH!

Termite sees a sign.

Ostrich and Termite fly.